Edward Thring

Poems and Translations

Edward Thring

Poems and Translations

ISBN/EAN: 9783337158231

Printed in Europe, USA, Canada, Australia, Japan

Cover: Foto ©Andreas Hilbeck / pixelio.de

More available books at **www.hansebooks.com**

Poems and Translations

BY

EDWARD THRING

Headmaster of Uppingham School, 1853–1887

London

T. FISHER UNWIN

26 PATERNOSTER SQUARE

MDCCCLXXXVII

THIS VOLUME OF VERSE IS DEDICATED

BY THE AUTHOR'S WISH

TO

Anna C. E. J. Koch

WHO THROUGH ALL HIS UPPINGHAM DAYS

MINISTERED TO HIM WITH A SISTER'S LOVE

PREFACE.

My Father had long wished to put out some work of his, which should be specially for the Boys of the School, past and present. It was suggested to him by a friend, that nothing could be better for this purpose than the School Songs, Borth Lyrics, and his other Poems, published in a small edition which all could buy, and which could be carried in a pocket. He took up the idea with great eagerness, and promised it should be his next work. The task of selecting and arranging them occupied him during his last summer holidays, spent at Birnam, in Perthshire, and he took the greatest trouble, that down to the smallest detail they should be fitting for the purpose for which he designed them. He desired to add to them, as a companion volume, the Addresses, which give some of his ideas on Teaching and Life-work. He sent his manuscripts to the publisher the day before he fell ill, having hastened their completion, as he was particularly anxious they should appear before the end of Term.

Knowing his great wish, I took up the task at once, and by the help of friends have been enabled to complete it in time.

SARAH E. THRING.

The Schoolhouse,

UPPINGHAM.

CONTENTS.

Dreamland.

Poems.

Hymns.

Translations.

I

DREAMLAND

THE BORDERLAND BETWEEN HEAVEN AND EARTH

[This Poem had its birth from holidays spent at Grasmere, and the conviction that noble dreams are great realities.]

DREAMLAND.

THE QUEEN.

Lo! afar,
'Neath the morning star,
Lies a hollow sweet and lone,
Girdled with an azure zone,
  Mountains sheer and steep,
  Massive walls of sleep,
  All round dim watch keep.

Heaven came down,
Kissed the mountain crown,
Soft his mantle round it laid,
Carved a holy space, and said,
  Be this magic round
  A soul garden-ground,
  In all life abound.

Never trees,
Never summer breeze,
Nor the sunny silent years,
Gleams of hope, and rainbow tears,
Wrought a fairer home,
Place to rest and roam
'Neath a living dome.

Jewelled rim
On a golden brim
Of a great cup, where the wine,
Gathered in its secret shrine,
Waiteth ages long,
Till some spirit strong
Pour it forth in song.

Here the Queen,
In dreamland sheen

Holds in her sky-woven bowers
Sceptred rule o'er dreamland hours.
Round her throne they stand,
Brothers hand in hand,
Lords of fair Dreamland.

Toil and strife,
All the seeming life,
Stricken heart, and stumblings blind,
Over, over, left behind.
Home the fleet years run,
Set free by the sun,
When their course is done.

Weary, spent,
From the slave-earth sent,
Lashed by burning rays of day,
On the threshold down they lay

Pain, and want, and tears ;
Happy, happy years,
Dreamland now is theirs.

There they lie
In the soft blue sky ;
And their life at will they pour
Gently backward or before :
By their own heart chime
Striketh dreamland time
In that happy clime.

In dreamland,
As they take their stand,
All sweet fancies round them rise,
In the summer of their eyes,
Palaces and towers,
Streamlets, elfin bowers,
As on earth spring flowers.

'Midst the hills

Which the love-glow fills,

At the music of sweet thought

Truth and bliss to shape are brought.

Hope, that scorn has chilled,

All that earth has killed,

Here new worlds doth build.

PILGRIMS OF EARTH.

FIRST PILGRIM.

Lost, lost, lost!

The sun out of the children's hearts is gone,

Their own clear sun is lost, which from them
  shone,

And turned to gold whate'er they looked upon :
  The children's sun is lost.

SECOND PILGRIM.

Lost, lost, lost!

The faith which through the meadows hand in
  hand

In cowslip days a happy future planned,

And tied sweet promises in cowslip band :
  The cowslips bloom no more.

THIRD PILGRIM.

Lost, lost, lost!

The bright defiant truth and eager hope

With some great ill in the great world to cope,

And carve the coming days with larger scope:

The truth and hope are lost.

FOURTH PILGRIM.

Lost, lost, lost!

The noble brotherhood secure within

From treason's taint and passion's foolish din,

For a good cause to strive, or lose, or win:

The lilies all are gone.

FIFTH PILGRIM.

Lost, lost, lost!

The warrior spirit, which at close of day

Betrayed, and wounded, weary, cast away,

In the lost battle still could stand at bay:

So is the battle lost.

CHORUS OF DREAMS.

MORTAL breath of death in life,
   Dreamlike shadows of a dream,
Sparks from chance flints in the night,
   That by chance hoofs smitten gleam.

Gleam, and pass away as pass
   Iron footfalls down the street,
And the darkness closes in
   On the smiting of the feet.

Smitten so ye live, O men,
   Ye who dreamlike shadows seem,
Come to us, your shadows leave,
   Be for ever what ye dream.

All of glory, all of good,

    Passes through our mystic gate ;

Fear not, the lost battle wins

    Dreamland infinite and great.

On, on, we pass.

What though the shadows lengthen as we
    tread !

They do but tell us, moving as we move,

That the great sun behind us is not dead,

    And we not lost his love.

On, on, we pass.

And voices, did'st not hear them ? far and nigh,

Now near, now far, old voices clearer grown,

The echoes, beaten out from days gone by,

    Still claim us as their own.

On, on, we pass.

Dreams, calling, calling, calling, did'st not
  hear ?

The wild wind hushed, earth's grating wheels
  stood still,

Dreams calling in my heart, more near, more
  near,

  Clear from yon evening hill.

On, on, we pass.

And still the shadows lengthen ; and the sun

Bears witness of himself.   A glory new

From yon bright summit shows, ere day is done,

  A land where dreams are true.

DREAMLAND.

(SCENE.—*Grasmere.*)

THE vain world rushes past,
And through and round,
Like leaves upon the blast,
Dead, withered, moving fast,
Nor recks of holy ground.
Lifeless unrest, random blown,
In a region not its own,
'Midst a glory all unknown.
 Somewhere, somewhere,
" Ye waters deep the secret keep,
Be silent, hill and glen."

'Twixt earth and skies
Fair Dreamland lies ;
    Somewhere, somewhere,
The lost hopes live again
    In fair Dreamland.
All things of immortal birth,
Rudely jostled off the earth,
Find fit home, and holy air
    In Dreamland,
    In Dreamland fair.
Here the mountains, every one,
Breathe a guardian spell ;
Lean them up against the sun,
    Giants sentinel,
Great dreams that their thrones have won.
In the midst an emerald cup
Holds a little tranquil mere;
And the mirrored water-dream,
Happy in the lowest place,

Rules the circumambient sphere

By the right of its sweet face,

Gathering in with simple grace

Every thought upon it thrown

To a beauty of its own.

—Grassy slopes and rocky rim—

Peace from clouds and sunlit blue

Wells up to the very brim,

Peace from earth, and flowers, and dew,

And the great hills drink it up,

Till the mountains gleam anew,

All their sides a shifting hue,

    With the overflow.

Peace above, and peace below,

Purple glooms, that pass and go,

    Strips of day,

Where the sun has lost his way,

Dreaming with the dreams that play

In and out the boulders grey

On each giant side

In fair Dreamland.

Peace, peace, far and wide,

A charmed circle, a shut door,

A holy shrine,

And peace upon the holy floor.

CHORUS OF DREAMS.

WHEN the green earth came rushing through
    the light,
    Light new created, on creation's morn,
And all the sons of God, with joyous shout,
    Shouted to see it, then, then we were born.

The thoughts of the Almighty spake in light ;
    And light and life with soft immortal power
Passed onward, and the invisible wave made sight
    In happy births, rock, river, tree, and flower.

Then blessed spirits saw the speech that lived
    In that great book laid open to their eyen,
And sight and truth were blended, one sweet
    tune,
    In myriad symphonies of thought Divine.

Wherever light and life are spread we live,

    Life's mighty angels ; but to man it seems,

With blind hands clutching light and finding

    none,

    That we are nothing, and he calls us dreams.

SUMMER VISITANTS.

THEY came here like the songbirds,
   With song, and joy, and game,
As songbirds from the snowland,
   Each merry year they came.

They came here as the bees come,
   Just where the sycamores
Spread broad their leaves, and cluster
   Their plumes round dreamland doors.

Ten summers long they came here,
   And then they came no more,
The sycamores were silent
   Around the dreamland door.

'Ten summers long they nestled,
  Then spread their wings and fled.
The sycamores were silent,
  As thus their love they said.

THE DREAMLAND HOME.

(Ben Place, 1877.)

WHAT happy spirit breathed upon thy birth,

Thou youngest child of Dreamland, foundling
    sweet,

In whom the charms of age and childhood meet,

Thou little plot of grass, dear ring of earth ?

Who gave thee thy twin lives ? one full of mirth,

The voice and dance of ever prattling rills,

One solemn with the silence of the hills;

Strange joy, strange peace, within thy tiny girth.

Thy whitewashed cottage 'neath its sycamore

Looks simple welcome; as a quiet face,

Bright with the halo of an inward store,

Breathes o'er uncomely features nameless grace,

The years unlock, old age his youth unfolds,

And hill with valley here child-happy revel holds.

(SCENE.—*Ben Place.*)

An old oak tree against the hill

    Leaned up its leafy crown ;

And, tumbling over rock and stone,

    A little beck ran down.

A pleasant thing it were to grow,

And let a thousand years or so

Throw all their summers at your feet.

Whilst gurgling in and out the spring,

A foolish, bright, wee, babbling thing,

Would make the old world young, heigho !

And as it babbled through the grass,

    A dream slipped down at eve,

Hung o'er the ripple like a mist,

    Its music to receive.

THE SONG OF THE BECK.

MOSS.

OH, the sky was bonny,
  Bonny, and bright, and gay,
Softly ran the water,
  Soft sang its roundelay.

Looked the sky on water,
  Water it looked on sky;
Sky and water married—
  I am their bairnie, I.

Softly ran the water,
  Soft is its life in me,
Bonny shone the blue sky,
  Purple and broiderie.

Slipped the brightness through me;
  Needles of glittering gold
Flicked me golden fringes,
  Feathered each feathery fold.

Spake the sky to water,
  Give me my bairnie wee;
Water answered blue sky:
  Nay, but that canna be.

You can come and go, ma'am,
  A lady of high degree,
I must run on errands,
  Leave the wee bairn to me.

So his cheeks I fondle,
  Stay with him running by,
Soft as softest water,
  Bright as the winsome sky.

Clothe the stones with softness,
  Bind up each rift and cleft,
Weave with busy finger
  Purple and golden weft.

My bright lady mother
  Gaily above may roam,
Still the water kisses
  His little stay-at-home.

THE MOTHER.

O MOTHER, dream thy dreams,
  Sing, sing thy lullaby;
Sing mother from dreamland
  The vision of thine eye.

THE DEWDROP.

SOFT a pulse of breathing
   Stirs a tiny sheet ;
Soft two drooping eyelids
   Soft eye-cushions meet.

Dropped a young boy angel,
   Sliding down the sky,
Saw the baby lying,
   Mother sitting by;

Stretched a sportive winglet,
   With his feather tips
Tickled baby heartstrings,
   Tickled baby lips.

Through the baby dewdrop
   Shot the angel gleam ;
And a smile celestial
   Broke from baby's dream.

Then the maiden dewdrop
   Waxed and grew the while,
Purest tints of heaven
   Mantled in her smile.

She on earth's dark forehead
   Shone a glorious thing,
Pearled with light celestial,
   Shadows of the wing.

Earth became a dreamland
   In the dewdrop ray,
In two worlds which claimed her,
   Passed she on her way.

THE FATHER.

O FATHER stout and strong,
  A little moment sped
Out of the battle throng
  To rest thy grey old head.

Dream on, and fight thy fight,
  Sound for thy gallant son,
Sound thy bold trump at night,
  For the lost battle won.

THE WATERFALL.

His young life
Drawn from the deep heart of the inner world,
Came clear and sparkling from the eternal hills,
Flowed through a boyhood gemmed with flowers
    and grass,
Song-visited, whilst o'er it gentle wings
Dropped little happy shadows on the pools,
Sweet memories of life that might not stay.
And so he grew to manhood, and was dashed
Over the rocks, and smitten down the chasms;
Then, in the blind clasp of the pitiless world,
Tossed to and fro betwixt the hard, smooth hate,
In the wild tumult of the torrent fall,
His soul, laid bare and stricken, showed the life

Churned into spray of noble thought, and sheets

Of whiteness.   All the glory, all the strength,

By busy hatred shattered in and out,

Leapt with a rush of light and onward power,

Snow-pure ; and o'er the misty tumbled deep

God laid His sunbow, and His peace came down,

And made the troubled waters breathe of peace.

A DREAM OF LIFE.

I.

CHILDE ROLAND wandered through the wood,
The old oak trees about him stood,
He thought them very old, heigho !

Through tufted grass and brambly spray
He wandered, on fresh flowers he lay,
His heart did many worlds enfold.

In sunshine chasing butterflies,
In shadeland closing happy eyes,
He dreamed his dreams, dreamed on, heigho !

A ladybird dropped from the sun,
The summer through his heart did run,
And all the world was summer gold.

II.

Childe Roland through the forest sped,
The forest answered to his tread
With tirila, with tirila.

Two boar-spears in his stout right hand,
Two gallant dogs at his command,
Rock, river knew him as their own.

The boar stood grimly in the way;
Childe Roland laughed; quoth he, " To-day
I'll teach him to sing tirila."

Childe Roland stood in the broad glade,
His gallant dogs about him played,
An oaken chaplet was his crown.

III.

King Carl sat on his throne so high,
Beneath, his kingdom's chivalry,
And trumpets sounding long, hurrah !

They charge, they wheel, on helm and shield
Rings battle, ha they yield, they yield !
In burst Roland, Roland.

To left and right swung back the fight,
Childe Roland laughed ; quoth he, " Smite,
    smite !
This warms the blood—hurrah ! "

They crowned him with a crown of gold—
Quoth he, " Sir King, the next I hold
Shall come from foeman's hand."

IV.

Sprang King Boabdil from his throne,
Childe Roland such a blast hath blown,
Down tumbled tower and town, heyda.

Childe Roland stood in the broad plain,
The Paynim spears, like driving rain,
Edged in dark scuds from end to end.

'Mid dust, and sun, and sobs of death,
Thick pantings, thirst, and furnace breath,
Quoth he, " The sport grows hot, heyda ! "

No hope ; they come ; quoth he then, " Nay,
Come now who will, we'll stand at bay—
One frank free hour at bay, my friend."

v.

Childe Roland leaned upon his sword
At eve, far off the Paynim horde
A dark ring round him glared, heigho !

Childe Roland blew upon his horn ;
Faint echoes, sad, betrayed, forlorn,
Came back alone, alone, alone.

Count Bertrand crept up to his feet,
With dying lips the Childe did greet ;
And all is lost—all lost, heigho !

" Nay," quoth Roland, " by God Most High !
We'll show the Paynim how men die,
In the lost battle we have won ! "

The sun went down, the moon came out
   Pale as a winding-sheet,
Saw Roland lying cold and stark,
   And Bertrand at his feet.

THE DREAM-RIVER.

Thou playfellow of boyhood,
　And manhood's living friend,
O tell us of thy rising,
　O tell us of thy end !

Speak, happy river, basking
　In glories from above ;
Speak, river, of thy gladness,
　Speak, river, of thy love.

Green trees may sigh for freedom,
　Tied down to common earth ;
And cornfields toil, and flowers
　Unseen be little worth.

But thou art free to follow
  The light of beauty's eyes,
Earth's pleasant shades to borrow,
  And brightness from the skies.

Unlock thy crystal chambers,
  Speak, every living wave,
Ere all love secrets perish
  Within the deep sea-grave.

I see the sun at morning,
  The moon come down at night,
And tell thee what I know not
  Of regions angel-bright.

Far, far, beneath thy waters
  Are purple clouds at play,
And flowers of earth peep downwards
  At others fair as they.

And wayward ripples sporting,
  Half vexed, and half at ease,
Play frolic hide and seeking
  With many a passing breeze.

Thine are all gentle secrets
  Of air, and sky, and earth,
Since first thy smiles were breaking
  In eddies at thy birth.

Check not thy magic gliding,
  Unriddle me no spell,
But flash on me the glances
  That lovers know full well.

Still let me gaze upon thee,
  Thou mirror of the skies,
And read the secret yearnings
  Of calm uplifted eyes.

Still learn in lowly pathways
To scatter life-dews sweet,
Nor lose in upwards gazings
The flowerets at my feet.

THE DREAM-BIRD.

THE broad bright day has sounds enough
　　Of busy, swarming strife ;
The wide faint air is forced to bear
　　The crush of noisy life.

One silver voice divides the reign
　　Of darkness with the moon ;
No other cry might dare to vie
　　With her pure liquid noon.

Soul of the night, that gathers up
　　The might of silent hours,
The awe of darkness, and the breath
　　Of sleeping lime-tree flowers.

To pour them forth a glowing tide
  Of strange wild music fire,
Half joy, half sadness, dark and light,
  Coy fear, and brimmed desire;

In thee the piercings of keen stars,
  The moonbeams, soft and pale,
Cool dews, and summer-haunted air
  Are speaking, Nightingale.

A PILGRIM OF EARTH.

O FOR for a little rest, rest for the weary brain,

Rest for the weary heart, rest for the ceaseless
  pain;

The pain of never knowing rest, the pain of the
  hunter's prey,

Whom the flying moments hunt and chase till
  he sinks with the dying day.

Sinks with the dying day, but finds no rest, no
  rest,

Lies and dreams he must up, and tosses sore
  distrest,

Lies and dreams he must fly, and, waking, flies
  hard prest;

Wakes and flies in his pain, and flying dreams
  of rest.

DREAMS.

AWAKE, awake, O Peace,
  Where, lying soft asleep,
The Moorhen and the silent Coot
  Shy watch around thee keep.

O leave the warbler in the sedge
  To sing her lullaby,
Leave thy smooth mirror, leave the bees,
  And open, Sweet, thine eye.

SONG OF THE TARN.

(SCENE.—*Loughrigg.*)

A LITTLE tarn beneath the hill,
    A jewel in the grass,
A little cup, where clouds and sun
    In gleams and shadows pass.

Methinks the mountains round have caught
    The blue sky and the rain,
And hid them in their heart of hearts,
    Then sent them up again :

To show to weary hearts that peace
    Beneath the rocks may dwell,
And bid them wait for light to come,
    Born in its stony well.

So nestling in its mountain home,

The child of earth and sky,

It lies beneath the hills, but yet

Looks up with loving eye.

DREAM SENTINEL ON THE MOUNTAIN.

(SCENE.—*The Langdales*.)

Ho, warder, to the rampart,
 The faint uncertain fall
Of weary human footstep
 Beats on the mountain wall.

Ho, warder, call the dream-clouds,
 Forth rolling cold and dim,
Loose all the phantom blindness
 Down o'er the rugged rim.

A leaden-coloured ocean,
 A mighty wand'ring plain,
That breaks in rifts and gathers,
 And breaks in rifts again.

While solemn still upraise them,
   In majesty serene,
Two mountain standard-bearers
   The parted deeps between.

A moment, adamantine
   The mighty bulwarks stay,
Then rolling dreams surge o'er them,
   In dreams they pass away.

Scoop out the hollow darkness,
   In moving vaults of night,
Then glitter in the blackness,
   And pass along the sight.

And out of the confusion
   Let great grey spectres gleam,
Rock, battlement, and boulder,
   To buttress up the dream.

Set fast each crag and mountain,
   Yet make them come and go,
That seeing, none may see them,
   And knowing, may not know.

Then where the cloud is thickest,
   And seethes the sea of white,
Portcullis all the gloaming
   With sweeps of downshot light.

Bar from the mystic portal
   Proud heart and stony head,
Yea, let them hug their treasure,
   But ne'er in Dreamland tread.

But if there come a dreamer,
   Ye dreams enfold your kin,
Thought touches thought in Dreamland,
   And float him gently in.

THE QUEEN.

COURAGE, here the Dreamland sun is shining,
　　Such as children's hearts,
Clear-orbed, perfect crystal, half divining,
　　Catch by fits and starts.

Hear the song of Truth through Dreamland
　　　　Stations
　　Sure, bright passage make;
As the sun were thinking, and the nations
　　Lived in light that spake.

Courage, here the sunny thoughts are flowing,
　　Rippling chimes of light,
Light that thinks aloud, a clear voice throwing
　　Down the fields of sight.

Banished hopes, and sighs from martyr prisons,
    Things of tender birth,
Eagle wings sore wounded, wistful visions,
    Battles lost on earth,

Prophet yearnings full of tearful seeing
    Bathe in summer here,
Till they rise resistless, launch their being
    On the golden year.

Courage, softly pulse the thought vibrations
    Up the dreamy stair,
Thought with thought in mazy undulations,
    Dreamer, come thou near.

Come where reigns our Queen; around her
    bending
    Dreams of fiery wing.
Watch, and wait the fated hour of sending;
    Watch, in act to spring.

THE DREAMS.

ROLL the mist from off his eyes,
Greet him with a glad surprise,
Let the light within him reach
To the utmost bounds of speech,
Wheresoever heart can find
Language sweet of life and mind,
Music of the rainbow's tears,
Unseen chiming of the spheres,
Hopes forgotten, tender wings
Of bright, happy, far-off things
That peeped forth to try the day,
Died on earth and flew away.
Let him see behind, before,
Dreams to come and dreams of yore,
Visions from Time's golden store ;
Time, the mighty pioneer,
Time, the earth-worm's word of fear,

Striding onward, axe in hand,

Clears the forest from the land,

Smites the old glooms where they stand,

Till there bloom a space, and then

All the sweet dreams live again—

Live, and flourish tender, true,

New-born in a world that's new.

Time, the mighty pioneer,

Bringing in the golden year,

Marches onward, axe in hand,

Smites the old glooms as they stand,

Thousand thousands round him throng,

Dreams the conquerors, the strong,

Matched against triumphant wrong :

Crushed, imprisoned, lonely pain,

Prophet yearnings banished, slain,

Wake, and come to life again.

Swept away till all is bare,

Silence in the empty air,

Void and silence everywhere,

Barren waste of barren air ;

Then they come like dropping dew

Out of nothing into view.

In a moment they are here,

And the gracious, tender throng,

Long expected, waiting long,

Takes possession ; earth is bright

With the showered dreamland light :

Not a little leaf but holds

A sweet thought within its folds ;

Every blade of grass is set

In a dreamland coronet :

Dreams soft dropping as the dew

Out of nothing into view.

Bring the weary pilgrim near,

Let him see the golden year,

Roll the mist from off his eyes,

Greet him with a glad surprise.

THE PILGRIM.

(SCENE.—*The Easedales.*)

AH me, ah me,
How sweet it is to be
A wave of life within a living sea,
To lie and feel
The new thoughts steal,
And rippling sound and light their tribute pour,
In life that thrills to life for evermore.

Yon mountain nigh
Spreads circling arms on high,
A great dream couched beneath a dreamy sky.
Rocks slant and gleam,
Whilst here a stream,

And there, runs down with happy message
    bright,
As hill to valley speaks in rushing light.

    The young fair earth,
    A blessed fairy birth,
Haunts this grey lap with peace and childlike
    mirth;
    A sportive grace,
    Like some sweet face,
Plays in and out and meets the loving eyes,
With ever changeful looks, and glad surprise.

    The purple glow
    Of heart-wealth from below
Wells up, and smiles are glancing to and fro
    Of light self-brought
    From inward thought.
Dim promises are moving, all the hills
Flush with joy-births and tender visible thrills.

A meadow fair

Holds breadths of quiet air

Beneath, and fronts the Ghyll down-leaping
there

In flakes that write

(Fair sheets of white),

The busy thoughts of yon still tarn, that lies

Watchful of all that moves in earth and skies.

But farther in,

Aside, the green slopes win

From the great mountains holier space between :

And everywhere

The jealous air

Keeps guard that nought go in but happy things,

No shadows fall, but waifs from angel wings.

A floating song,

The pensive vale along

Runs down, a stream of gentle life, and strong.

Who stand there feel

Their senses steal

Into the flood which goes on singing still,

And still the empty heart with light doth fill.

A great dream throne,

What seems a silent stone,

Stands 'midst the water's mystic undertone,

A fragment tost,

From old worlds lost,

And on it one still form keeps lonely state,

And that weird valley rules by dreamland fate.

Here throng the dreams,

Naught only what it seems,

The stream it dreameth, and the flowers are

dreams.

Yon starry spells

Are asphodels,

The sundew dreams its scarlet, tiny elves
Weave moss, and run along the river shelves.

They rush apace
With fine fantastic grace,
And the wild valley fills with ferny lace ;
They round the air
To bluebells fair,
Breathe in the very grass, and, like a stream,
Change evermore, but still unchanging seem.

My eyes are clear,
They see the Dream Queen near,
And the still valley nurse the golden year ;
The air rolls back,
The spirit track
Lies open ; lo, they come ! how sweet to be
A living wave within a living sea !

POEMS.

POEMS.

AIR.

WHO art thou, thou softest one, bright queen of
    earth and ocean,
  Summer's bride, that on the sunny grass
Sleep'st unseen, so gently, without motion ?
  All creation waits for thee to pass.

Thou uprisest, and thy lieges bow them down
    before thee.
  Music bursts from forest, dale, and hill ;
All the earth is strung with light and glory ;
  At thy touch its myriad harpstrings thrill.

Wayward Being, dancing with the happy maids
    at even ;
  Dancing, till awakes thy jealous pride ;
Then amongst them, in thy beauty stealing,
  Thou hast stabbed the fairest in her side.

Smiling thou did'st stab her, and she flushed,
    and wasted slowly ;
  Then thou strewest flowerets on her grave,
All remorseful, chanting soft and lowly,
  While the grasses in the churchyard wave.

Soon forgetful with the lark thou warblest high
    in heaven,
  Rolling with the rolling clouds in play,
Changeful, down thou dartest, passion driven,
  Swooping with the eagle on its prey.

Thee the sailor prays for, on the broad Pacific
    lying,
  When like molten fire glows the sea,
And the fierce sun keeps him long a-dying ;
  Then he thinks of home, and prays for thee.

Sweet the balmy breath of hay on summer
    morns, dew-laden,
  Sweet the rose, most sweet the eglantine,
Song of birds, and whispered vow of maiden,
  All sweet things of sound and scent are
    thine.

In us, round us, over us, yet closed to feeble
    mortals,
  Where we live, but pass not till we die,
Gnat and insect open find thy portals,
  Thou'rt a world of gladness to the fly !

Mighty queen, thy sceptre rules in forest, plain,
  and mountain—
  Wheresoever earth is found, or sea,
Down in sunless caves, 'neath stream and
  fountain,
  All things living draw their life from thee.

THE FOUNTAIN OF YOUTH.

THE SCHOOL.

THE summer came, a floating song
　　Upon a sea of gold.
The sun-thoughts ran along the slopes,
　　And settled where they wold.
And somewhere up, far in the sky,
　　In happy angel play,
The gates of bliss have lifted been,
　　And flooded all the day.

And know ye not where round about
　　The summer's mystic well
The Hours are brought to drink at morn,
　　At eve come back to dwell.

Youth starts at dawn, and oft again,
　　Returning, thinks to find
The merry little fool he left,
　　In days long past, behind.

Lo, where three hundred years have crowned
　　Its grey, old, honoured head,
Just as a mountain rivulet
　　Clasped in a stony bed,
The school-house sees from hour to hour
　　The schoolboy's rippling feet,
With laugh, and song, and quip, and jest,
　　Go hurrying down the street.

Deep pools there are, where that bright
　　　　stream
　　All calm and open lies,
When silent faces catch a gleam
　　Of God from out the skies ;

And ever 'midst the kneeling ranks
   Some hero in Christ's name
Draws secret breath, and sees o'erhead
   Christ's living banner flame.

Still like a mountain rivulet,
   Clasped in its stony bed,
Flow through these walls from hour to hour
   The schoolboys' rippling tread,
And youth and age still love to meet
   Round Summer's mystic well,
Where age grows young, and youth rings out
   A joyous passing bell.

IN MEMORIAM.

MRS. EWING.

ALL in the dusty camp she stood,
  A queen by queenly right ;
The sunbeams made her diadem,
  Her parted lips breathed light.

She spake the words none else might speak,
  And sweet new life from far
Came down in rippling waves of joy,
  As from some happy star.

The bugles, like the silver call
  Of God's own trumpets, rang ;
The very dust to diamonds turned,
  And forth her heroes sprang.

Then changed she to a twilight strain,
  So sad, so softly bright ;
Sweet death, sweet life, dissolved in tears,
  Each tear an orb of light.

So wept they, as on summer eves
  Fall fast the dews that bless ;
Old oak and bladed grass alike
  Wax strong in tenderness.

Then passed she ; but the joy still floats
  O'er camp and soldier lad,
Thrills through the bugles, eyes still weep
  Bright tears all blissful-sad.

So passed she, but the mystic light
    So far, so near,
Shines on, shines on,
    From Paradise,
Where she is gone, where she is gone.

THE OLD BOYS' MATCH.

" CRABBED age and youth
   Cannot live together."
Poet, tell the truth
   In the summer weather.

Youngest welcome rung
   Out of grey old gables,
Old Boys all were young,
   Whispered old young fables.

So we met, and played,
   Young and old together;
Merry work we made.
   Poet, keep your tether.

A CAGE DREAM.

FRIEND over the sea,
  Free as the eye to roam,
Singeth a song to me,
  Prisoned and pent at home :
    " I'll come out to thee,
        Friend over the sea."

'Tis but a dream, I know ;
  Yet, though it may not be,
Nay, I shall never go,
  Singeth a dream to me :
    " I'll come out to thee,
        Friend over the sea."

Friend over the sea,
   Free as the eye to roam,
Singeth my bird to me,
   Still in my heart at home ;
         Happy, though caged he be,
            Still coming to thee.

NEW WALLS.

SLOW rose of breathed adamant the wall
Of Troy, as wave on wave of charmed sound
Hung, crystal fixed, the holy centre round,
Close-bonded light and music girding all.
So on the old school came a spirit call,
Stirred the deep harp which thrice a hundred
    years
Had strung with all their gladness, all their
    tears,
Made light and faith in living music fall.
Then rose the strong foundations; to the sound
Of ghostly chant, and angel whispers, grew
Tier upon tier of melody spellbound,
To last while lasts the heavenly strain. O you,
Who dwell within the circle, wiser found,
Cheat not the immortal Builder of His due.

THE SILVER WEDDING.

Ah me ! how men, in weary days of old,
E'en as they hardened, backward glances threw ;
And sad, weird women murmured, " It is true,
" To iron turns the age of virgin gold."
And Time's grey wings all beauty do enfold,
Make grey the tattered trees, sweep grey the
    skies,
Chill the sweet breath of summer into sighs ;
And earth, a grey old crone, blinks in the cold.
But a fresh cycle comes, new Edens rise
Out of this iron age, as hand in hand,
In God's dear presence man and maiden stand
And heavenly alchemy its secret tries.
The silver wedding first, as Time takes hold
With Love ; and fifty years bring back the gold.

OLD AGE.

AND age is winter. I am growing old ;
Grey hairs have long since straggled into place,
And feet, once winged jests, that laughed to race,
Plod slow and halting, like a tale ill-told.
What though the frost upon the roof lay hold,
'Tis a poor house whose battered frame the wind
Can whistle through at will, and roomage find,
Whose bankrupt tenant all his goods hath sold !
But warm and bright Old Christmas sits at home,
Keeps mirthful house with noise of dance and
    jest,
Or silence sweeter still, when feet that roam
Meet round his hearth once more, and gather
    rest.
Let thriftless summer lightly come and go,
Old age hath steadier fires at his command that
    glow.

Hymns.

HYMNS.

WRITTEN FOR THE NORMAL SCHOOL, ST. CLOUD, MINNESOTA, U.S.

(March 19, 1887.)

WHITHER away, whither away?
When the dew is on the thorn,
    And the silvery grass
Shakes off happy gleams of morn
    As the light feet pass,
Whither away, O, whither away?

I.

We have gathered seeds of light
Dropped on old Time's mountain height,
As the new day came in sight.

II.

Heralds of the light are we,

Sowers of the world to be,

With a seed light, pure, and free.

III.

Heralds of the morn we stand,

Foot to foot, and hand in hand,

Flinging morning o'er the land.

IV.

Honour from yon morning star

O'er the lonely grave afar,

Which the pioneer did bar.

Minnesota, Minnesota, joyous and true.

Whither away, whither away?

When the dew is on the thorn,

And the silvery grass

Shakes off happy gleams of morn

As the light feet pass,

Whither away, O, whither away?

v.

Seeds of light we scatter round,

Wisdom, knowledge, song seeds, found

In Time's great old hunting ground.

VI.

Dreams, that o'er life's restless mass,

As the wind o'er prairies, pass,

Bending hearts as bends the grass;

VII.

Purest love from forests deep,

Where the lone backwoodsmen keep

Memories that never sleep.

VIII.

Light and life we scatter round,

Maiden truth, pure manhood, found

In Time's great old hunting ground.

Minnesota, Minnesota, joyous and true.

HOPE.

Queen of men, whose lowly birth is
    Half of mercy, half of sin,
Queen of men, wherever earth is,
    And a heaven above to win ;
Yet thou wert not a guest in Paradisan bowers,
Nor couldest find a resting-place amongst those
    flowers.

Gift of God, at Eden's portals
    Shrinking from the flaming sword,
Down descending with us mortals,
    Sinless, yet with sin's award ;
Heaven owns thee not, yet still of heaven thou
    art,
Earth-born, yet still of heaven our sole remain-
    ing part.

Baby form 'mid curses cradled,
  Born to slavery and death,
Faint thy sorrow-laden mother,
  When thou first wert drawing breath ;
Yet when she saw thee, smiling through her
  tears,
Almost she then forgot the woe that made thee
  hers.

Wayward spirit, sinking, rising,
  Floating on sky-woven wings,
Life's twin sister, half despising
  Her, and all earth-living things,
Yet thou hast sunk low down full near where
  Hell begins,
But Hell's no place for thee, thy foot still up-
  wards springs.

Earth-cold vapours cling around thee,
  Borrow brightness from the sun ;

On though mid-day fires confound thee,
    Evening closes, it is done.
Yet after all thy pains, like an unwary fly,
Doomed in excess of light to pass heaven's gates
    —and die.

Children see thee holding roses
    Just before them as they run,
Or on purple hills reposing,
    Garlanded with evening sun ;
Roses thou hast for children, but a sword for
    men,
To win what men have dared, and yet shall dare
    again.

Thy light angel wings are fanning
    Sleeping infants into smiles,
With the old man thou art planning
    Death-deluding holy wiles ;

Youth thinks thee all his own, and clasps thee
    to his side,
Yet thou can crown grey hairs with more
    enduring pride.

    Leader of the Martyr armies,
      Not the least of those blest three,
    Envying not to Faith her wonders,
      Her great place to Charity;
Content to leave to them what richer profit
    seems,
So thou may'st revel on in thy own glorious
    dreams.

    When the sun had gathered blackness,
      And the stars were sick and dim,
    Veiled before a dying Saviour,
      Fainting as they looked on Him,

Then in that dread eclipse thy eyes alone were
    bright,
Streaming through darkened worlds the fulness
    of their light.

    Lead me, for I fain would follow,
      Struggle onwards still with me,
    From Faith journey-money borrow,
      Comfort ask of Charity.
With the first sigh of grief thou stoodest by my
    side,
On my last dying breath toward Heaven trium-
    phant ride.

DEATH.

DEATH shut the gates of Paradise
  'Gainst Adam and his sin,
And forged of flames the turning sword
  That barred the pathway in ;

But ever since, to check his pride,
  Man's servant has he been,
Sits sadly at the doors of life,
  And toils to let us in.

GOOD-NIGHT.

A DAY of work is done,
  I needs must lay me down,
Lord, when the battle's won,
  Grant me a victor's crown.

When life's long day is past,
  So may I sink to rest;
Sweet be my sleep at last,
  And with the present, blest.

HE THAT WAS DEAD SAT UP.

ST. LUKE vii. 15.

GREAT GOD! Thou God of David, lo!
What voice, more soft than tears that flow,
Down from Thy throne descended;
What silence of Archangel wings
Made space, as to the dead it brings
Thy life, and death is ended!
The living, yea! the living, praise
Thy Name, the living glory raise.

Hosanna! Jesu, David's son!
Hosanna! Jesu, promised one:
Thou, who the dead hast saved.
Rise, Star of Jacob, rise and shine;
Smite, Son of David, earth is thine;
Sit on the throne of David.
What silence of Archangel swords
Sweeps watchful round Thee, Lord of lords!

8

LORD, HAVE MERCY ON ME.

LORD, have mercy on me, humble
All my being unto Thee ;
As a silent snow-flake melting
Into heaven's translucent sea ;
Where before the throne of glory
Deeps of pure humility
Ever lie outstretch'd before Thee,
Spirit-flashing shrines to be.

Humble all my soul within me,
Make my spirit clear and bright ;
As a dewdrop in the morning
Animate with living light,
Till the earthy tie dissolving,
Death shall gently set me free,
Passing, as a silent snow-flake,
Into heaven's translucent sea.

A CHRISTMAS CAROL.

FLASHING through the Eastern night,
Tides of music and of light
Tell the shepherds it is dawn,
Ere the sun has brought the morn :
Dawn of life that never dies,
Day in night for praying eyes.

Day in night, and life in death,
Ushered in by angel breath,
New creation, earth and sea
Glowing with the life to be,
And the Lord of Glory known,
With the manger for a throne.

Clouds can change to light, new-born,

With a soul of fire at morn ;

And the great sun is a guest

Cradled in the dewdrop's breast.

Lo ! the King—a babe, on earth :

Nought but has a second birth.

Happy life in homes, each one

Lighted by its own clear sun ;

Happy life, where angel feet

Duly tread the dreary street :

Happy life, where children play ;

Stars that twinkle all the day.

Praise Him, all ye poor, who bear

Hearts at peace in troubled air :

Praise Him, ye who live within

Charmed circles, free from sin ;

Islands in the sea of woe,

Where the wild winds come and go.

Lo! the King! a babe, alone,

With the manger for a throne.

Praise Him, angels, chant again

Peace on earth, goodwill to men.

Praise Him, happy living things,

Lord of Life, and King of kings.

HYMN FOR THE NATIVITY.

HAPPY night, and happy silence downward
    softly stealing,
  Softly stealing over land and sea,
Stars from golden censers swung a silent, eager
    feeling
  Down on Judah, down on Galilee;
And all the wistful air, and earth, and sky,
Listened, listened for the gladness of a cry.

Holy night, a sudden flash of light its way is
    winging;
  Angels, angels, all above, around;
Hark! the angel voices, hark! the angel voices
    singing;
  And the sheep are lying on the ground.

Lo! all the wistful air, and earth, and sky,

Listen, listen to the gladness of the cry.

Happy night at Bethlehem; soft little hands
    are feeling,

  Feeling in the manger with the kine,

Little hands, and eyelids closed in sleep, while
    angels kneeling,

  Mary mother, hymn the Babe divine.

Lo! all the wistful air, and earth, and sky,

Listen, listen to the gladness of the cry.

Wide, as if the light were music, flashes
    adoration :

  " Glory be to God, nor ever cease."

All the silence thrills, and speeds the message
    of salvation:

  " Peace on earth, goodwill to men of peace."

Lo l all the wistful air, and earth, and sky,

Listen, listen to the gladness of the cry.

Holy night, thy solemn silence evermore
  enfoldeth
Angel songs and peace from God on high;
Holy night, thy watcher still with faithful eye
  beholdeth
Wings that wave, and angel glory nigh.
Lo! hushed is strife in earth, and air, and sky;
Still thy watchers hear the gladness of the cry.

Praise Him, ye who watch the night, the silent
  night of ages;
  Praise Him, shepherds, praise the Holy
  Child;
Praise Him, ye who hear the light, O praise
  Him, all ye sages;
  Praise Him, children, praise Him, meek and
  mild.
Lo! peace on earth, glory to God on high!
Listen, listen to the gladness of the cry.

TRANSLATIONS.

Translations.

OLD GERMAN.[1]

Dayspring of eternal day,
  Light from depths of light unending,
Flash on us this dawn Thy ray,
  Bright gleams on our faces sending ;
Chase, O chase through Thy great might
      All our night.

Let Thy kindly morning dew,
  On our weary hearts down-falling,
Life's dry, withered sod renew,
  Pure, sweet trust and health recalling ;
Quicken us, Thy sons of yore,
      Evermore.

[1] Uppingham School Hymn Book.

Grant Thy love with cleansing fire
   Burn out all our cold works' deadness ;
Kindle soul and heart's desire
   In th' uprisen morning redness,
That we, ere we set in night,
      Stand upright.

O Thou Dayspring from on high,
   Grant that, when the last day shineth,
We may rise again to fly
   Where none vexeth or repineth,
Finding in that happy place
      Joy and grace.

Sun of Blessing, lift Thy face,
   Light us in Thy glorious keeping,
Guide us into that sweet place,
   Through this vale of tears and weeping,
Where the bliss, that thrills on high,
      Ne'er shall die.

FROM THE GERMAN OF J. RIST.[1]

ETERNITY, thou word of fear,

O Sword, that through the soul doth shear,

    O Dawn, that knows no setting.

Endless duration, time no more,

I wot not where, bewildered sore,

    To turn, all ways forgetting.

My terror-stricken heart doth heave,

And to my gums my tongue doth cleave.

O God, Thou righteous Judge, how strait

Upon the wicked man do wait

    Thy judgments unrelenting.

Alas! must man sin's little day

Through all eternity repay?

    Bethink Thee, Lord, repenting.

[1] Uppingham School Hymn Book.

Look to it, man, draw in thy breath,
How short is time, how quick is death !

Wake up, O man, from sinful sleep,
Arouse thyself, O poor lost sheep,
    Amend, and live more truly.
Wake up, the time is almost o'er,
Eternity is at the door
    To pay thy wages duly.
Perchance this sun lights thy last day,
For who can tell, when die he may ?

Eternity, thou word of fear,
O Sword, that through the soul doth shear,
    O Dawn, that knows no setting.
Endless duration, time no more,
I wot not where, bewildered sore,
    To turn, all ways forgetting.
Yet take me, when it pleaseth Thee,
Lord Jesus, in Thy joy to be.

FROM THE GERMAN OF PAUL GERHARD.[1]

Now woods their rest are keeping,
Men, cattle, fields are sleeping,
  The whole world lies in sleep.
But, O my soul, awaken,
Take heed, with faith unshaken,
  Thy great Creator's will to keep.

Now day is past and ended,
And golden stars ascended
  Shine forth in yon blue dome.
E'en so shall I, uprisen
From out of earth's sad prison,
  At last hear God's voice call me home.

[1] Uppingham School Hymn Book.

My eyes are drooping slowly,
And soon will close them wholly,
   Where shall the soul then dwell ?
Do Thou, O God, receive it,
Of all misdeeds relieve it,
   Thou light and ward of Israel.

Breathe, loved ones, peace and blessing ;
Mischance or aught distressing,
   Shall not come nigh your head.
Rest, loved ones, sweetly sleeping,
God's hosts their guard are keeping,
   And golden arms watch round your bed.

FROM THE GERMAN OF J. RIST.[1]

O GRIEF, O woe,
O deep heartblow,
Is not there cause for crying :
God the Father's only Son
In the grave low lying.

O wonder dread,
God's own Son dead,
Upon the cross death slew Him.
Love has won for us the throne,
Heaven ours is through Him.

O man, thy sin
The cause hath been,
This coil is all thy doing :
Since thou through thy evil deed
Wroughtest utter ruin.

[1] Uppingham School Hymn Book.

Thy bridegroom fair
Lies bleeding there,
The Lamb of God sore stricken :
He His life-blood meekly shed,
Thee in death to quicken.

O sacred face,
O fount of grace,
So spitefully entreated :
Naught on earth but would with tears
Thee perforce have greeted.

O Jesu best,
My shield, my rest,
I with tears beseech Thee :
Make me love Thee to the grave,
Then at last to reach Thee.

LUTHER'S HYMN.[1]

A FORTRESS strong is God our God,
A sword and shield around us,
His help us frees from all our woe,
What ill soe'er has found us;

 The old arch-traitor still,
 Bent to work his will,
 Might and craft hath girt,
 Dread armour to our hurt;
There's none on earth can match him.

Our might is naught, we naught have done,
All lost, of strength forsaken,
For us God's own incarnate Son,
True man, the field hath taken.

[1] Uppingham School Hymn Book.

And dost thou ask who came ?

Christ Jesus His name ;

Lord of Hosts, yea see,

None else is God but He,

He holds the field for ever.

Though full of devils were the world,

Hell ready us to swallow,

We will not be so sore afraid,

For sure, good end will follow ;

And though this world's prince set

Himself grimly, yet

Naught he can do now,

For he is judged, I trow,

One little word can quell him.

The word of God they must let stand

Perforce, 'tis not their merit,

Lo, He is ever at our hand,
With all His gifts and spirit.

What, and though they take life,

Honour, wealth, child, wife,

Let go, let them go !

No triumph do they know ;

For us stands fast the kingdom.

CHRISTMAS CAROL.[1]

(From the German.)

PEACEFUL night ! all things sleep,
Holy night ! lone watch keep
Still and wakeful the thrice bless'd pair.
Holy child with the clustering hair,
 Slumber in heavenly peace,
 Slumber in heavenly peace.

[2] Holy night ! stars above
Watch and wind sleepless in love,
O'er his cradle the glad vigils share.
Holy child with the clustering hair,
 Slumber in heavenly peace,
 Slumber in heavenly peace.

[1] School Songs.
[2] The second and third Stanzas are original.

Peaceful night ! glory on high,

Peace on earth angels cry,

Softly listens the wondering air.

Holy child with the clustering hair,

    Slumber in heavenly peace,

    Slumber in heavenly peace.

CHORALE FROM BACH'S CHRISTMAS ORATORIO.

O JESU babe, O Jesu mine,

Make Thee a cradle white and fine,

Come, rest Thee close in my heart shrine,

That I forget not, I am Thine.

FROM THE GERMAN OF

GRIMELSHAUSEN'S "SIMPLICISSIMUS."

1669.

COME, nightingale, thou soul of night,
Come in thy very sweetest plight,
  And set thy joy a-ringing.
Come, come, thy Maker praise, while all
The other birds a-sleeping fall,
  And must give over singing.
    Ring, ring, ting,
    Ring, throat, best of all outpouring
    Strains adoring,
    Glory give to God the Highest,

What though the day is gone, and we
Must all in darkness shrouded be,
   We ne'theless can be singing.
How good is God ! how great His might !
Nought reck we of the blinding night,
   To Him all glory bringing.
      Ring, ring, ting,
      Ring, throat, best of all outpouring
      Strains adoring,
      Glory give to God the Highest.

Echo's wild beat, and wandering voice,
Must needs be with us, and rejoice,
   And add her own sweet numbers.
She chases weariness away,
Which aye besets us day by day,
   And cheats us of our slumbers.

Ring, then, ring,
Ring, throat, best of all outpouring
Strains adoring,
Glory give to God the Highest.

The stars that stand up in the sky,
They turn to God with reverent eye,
  To give Him honour duly.
Yea, e'en the owl, who cannot sing,
What time his nightly hootings ring,
  Has learnt to praise Him truly.
    Ring, then, ring,
    Ring, throat, best of all outpouring
    Strains adoring,
    Glory give to God the Highest.

Up, then, dear birdie, up, I say,
We will not laziest be, nor stay
  In sleepy slumber lying.

Far rather till the morning red
O'er fieriest wilds its joyance shed,
   Our praise we will be plying.
      Ring, then, ring,
      Ring, throat, best of all outpouring
      Strains adoring,
      Glory give to God the Highest.

DU BIST DIE RUH'.

(From the German of Rückert, " Du bist die Ruh', der
Friede mild.")

OF gentle peace thou art the calm,

Love's pain art thou, and thou love's balm ;

I tender, full of joy and smart,

A home to thee, my eyes, my heart,

My eyes, my heart.

Turn in to me, and evermore

Shut after thee the silent door.

All other pain O banish quite,

Be my heart fill'd with thy delight,

With thy delight.

This orbèd eye, a home made bright

By thee alone, O fill it quite !

O fill it quite !

GOOD-NIGHT.

(From the German of Emanuel Geibel.)

Now dusky shades are falling,
   The shepherd moon on high,
To his cloud lambkins calling,
   Breathes forth his lullaby;
And still he sings so lowly,
Whilst starry voices holy
   My ear float softly by:
Slumber and rest, slumber and rest,
   The day is gone by and its rout,
Slumber and rest, slumber and rest,
The love of God shields close your nest,
   Shields close your nest all round about.

And now when 'neath the darkness
   The last pale tapers die,
The swarming cares are silent
   Which in the broad day fly;
The pine trees sigh sweet meaning,
And soft, forgetful dreaming
   Drops from the happy sky:
Slumber and rest, slumber and rest,
   The day is gone by and its rout,
Slumber and rest, slumber and rest,
The love of God shields close your nest,
   Shields close your nest all round about.

Good-night, then, weary numbers,
   Ye loved ones far and nigh;
I too have peaceful slumbers
   Till gleams the morning sky,
The nightingale, she only
Sings to the moon all lonely,
   And praises God most High:

Slumber and rest, slumber and rest,

The day is gone by and its rout,

Slumber and rest, slumber and rest,

The love of God shields close your nest,

Shields close your nest all round about.

MORGENLIED.

(From the German, "Erwacht in neuer Stärke.")

I WAKE with new strength gifted,
  O God, Thy light I greet ;
With happy face uplifted,
  Thy glorious works to meet.
How gay the sun shoots forth his fire,
And wakes up all life's clear-voiced quire !

Exultant song unending
  Bursts on air, thicket, lawn ;
From forest aisles, soft blending,
  Comes balmy breath of dawn.
The little birds shake off the dew,
Fly up, and sing in clearest blue.

The sun his course doth measure,
  And higher conquest makes ;
All living things breathe pleasure,
  And all that sleeps awakes.
O God, Thy sunlight shining free,
How glorious 'tis alive to be !

WANDERER'S NACHTLIED.

(From the German of Goethe, " Über allen Gipfeln
ist Ruh.")

On the hills is rest all around,
No wind is in the treetops found,
 Scarce breathes the air.
Birds all are silent ;
Mute on the green bough ;
Wait awhile, weary one, e'en thou
 Shalt rest thee fair.

DER TOD UND DAS MÄDCHEN.

(From the German of Claudius,
" Vorüber ! ach, vorüber, geh' wilder Knochenmann !")

PASS by me, O pass by me, grim skeleton, away!

I am but young, Sweet, leave me, O touch me
 not to-day!

Nay, give thy hand, thou fair and tender thing,
 Thy friend, I come not to molest thee.

Be of good cheer, I am not grim, soft in my
 arms wilt sleep, and rest thee.

SEHNSUCHT.

(From the German of Droysen, " Fern und ferner
schallt der Reigen.")

FAR, far sounds life's grand dance ever;
Ah me! silence me doth sever,
　　Everywhere.
Only to the full heart here
Cometh peace, ah! never.

Hark! the night o'er space is hieing,
Her robes rustle, softly sighing
　　Through the trees.
E'en so passion-tost like these,
Dreams through me are flying.

FAREWELL, THOU NOBLE WOOD.[1]

(From the German.)

AND so we part with joy and song,
　Farewell, thou noble wood,
Cool dells and dreamy branches,
Deep moss-enfolded trances ;
　To rest here aye, how good !

We chant to thee, as home we go,
　A hymn of gratitude,
Again invite us hither,
With songs and glad May weather,
　And balmy breath, fair wood.

Oh, see from far, the old wood hears
　Each twilight-haunted dell,
The little sprays nod greeting,
And voicèd tendrils meeting,
　Are murmuring farewell.

[1] School Songs.

DIE POST.

(From the German, "Von der Strasse her ein Posthorn
klingt.")

HARK! the Postman's horn from out the street!
What ails thee, so to leap up and beat,
   My heart?

The Post no letter brings for thee,
What means then this strange mutiny,
   My heart?

Ah! but the Post has come from where
She lives, my dearest darling fair;
   My heart.

Willst then, pray, go across and see,
And ask how all things there may be,
   My heart?

.

MAY SONG.

(From the German of Hölty.)

MAY is coming, dance to meet her,
  May, bright lady, winsome queen ;
May returning, magic splendour
  Sheds on hill and valley green,
Sweet spells breathing youth and bridal,
  Through wild woods and all they rule,
In the green blade's tender twilight,
  And the deepest, stillest pool.

Dance, young maiden, dance, sweet maiden,
  Sweeter, breathed upon by May ;
Thy clear ringing music blending
  With the morning bells at play.

Murm'ring with the murm'ring leaflets,
  With the nightingale rejoice;
Babbling sweet of hope and gladness
  Till young Echo wakes his voice.

Come, then, leave the smoky city,
  Joy and hope are calling thee;
Breathe, young maiden, happy May-time,
  From fresh breezes blowing free.
Come, put on your gipsy bonnet,
  Quick o'er flower-enwoven grass,
May, sweet May-time, lightly carol,
  Weave the fresh buds as you pass.

WITH HIS BOW AND ARROWS

(From the German of Schiller.)

WITH his bow and arrows,
Over hill and dale,
Comes the jolly bowman,
Bids the morning hail.

High in air the falcon
Rules with lordly wing;
Over glen and mountain
Is the archer king.

Far as eye can measure,
Far as arrow flies,
Is his realm; whatever
Soars or runs, his prize.

THE TWO HARES.

(From the German.)

'TWIXT the hill and shady, shady glen,
    Once there sat two hares O,
Cropp'd away the greenest, greenest grass,
    Cropp'd it, cropp'd it bare O.

After both full stuffing, stuffing, stuffing,
    O, ho! down they squatted,
Until the sportsman, sportsman came,
    Came and down them shotted.

When they then had pick'd the pieces all up,
    And eke their wits O,
Finding some little, little life left,
    Off they ran full split O.

PRINCE EUGENIUS.

(From the German.)

PRINCE EUGENE, that noble knight, sir,
Would algates for th' Emperor seize on
  Town and fortress of Belgrade ;
So across a bridge soon threw he,
And eftsoons his army drew he
  Straight the town for to invade.

When as then the bridge was ready,
Troops with bag and baggage led he
  Boldly o'er the Danube stream.
Soon he pitched his camp at Semlin,
Turks to hunt, of purpose steady,
  To their great disgrace and teen.

'Twas on the twenty-first of August,

Came a scout in thro' rain and raw gust,

   The prince he swore to and told him then,

That the Turks the country plunder

Much as may be guess'd, not under

   Thrice a hundred thousand men.

Prince Eugenius heard it all, sir,

Straight he bade together call, sir,

   His generals and field-marshals.

So he did advise them rarely,

Troops to lead on soft and fairly,

   On the foeman for to fall.

To their saddles climb'd they lightly,

Each gripp'd to his sword full knightly;

   In dead silence they advance.

Musketeers and troopers spurring,

All did deeds of gallant daring,

   'Twas, good sooth, a pretty dance.

Sergeants, in the van advancing,
Strike up for our ball and dancing,
  With your cannon great and small.
Great and small together strike up,
Pounding Turks and heathen quite up,
  Strike up till they scamper all.

Prince Eugene was on the right, sir,
Like a lion in the fight, sir,
  As general and field-marshal.
Prince Louis, he rode up and down O,
German brothers, keep your ground O,
  Steady, boys, charge home, set on.

Prince Louis he must eke surrender
His young life and spirit tender,
  Forced by cruel lead to die.
Prince Eugene was troubled sorely,
For he loved him so entirely,
  Had him brought to Peterwardein.

DAS SCHIFFLEIN.

(From the German of Uhland, " Ein Schifflein zichet
leise.")

A BOAT, the ripple cleaving,

Sped on, a smooth path leaving.

All silent sat, none greeting,

Each for the first time meeting.

Lo, the swart woodman looses

His wallet, and produces

A horn, that, soft notes flinging,

Set all the banks a-ringing.

Another, up and doing,

His trusty staff unscrewing,

Made flute tones clear onstealing

Blend with the horn's fierce pealing.

Without a word the maiden
Sat shyly, silence-laden,
Then in chimed she a-singing
To flute and horn wild ringing.

The rowers stirred with pleasure,
Took stroke for stroke the measure.
On flew the vessel bounding,
To song and music sounding.

In ran the boat high stranded,
They parted, all fair landed.
" Shall we on one ship, brother,
Again e'er meet each other ? "

www.ingramcontent.com/pod-product-compliance
Lightning Source LLC
Chambersburg PA
CBHW021132020726
47500CB00003B/1048